Title Withdrawn

YUMMY
LITTLE
COOKBOOK

Rebecca Gilpin and Catherine Atkinson

Designed by Non Taylor and Amanda Gulliver
Illustrated by Non Taylor, Molly Sage, Kim Lane and Sue Stitt
Photographs by Howard Allman
Cover design by Hannah Ahmed
Edited by Fiona Watt

American editor: Carrie Seay   American expert: Barbara Tricinella

Contents

CHOCOLATES & CANDIES

Beside each ingredients list, you can find out how long the chocolates and candies will keep. If you give them as a present, make sure you also tell the person you are giving them to. In lots of the recipes, you will use teaspoons and tablespoons for measuring. Use measuring spoons if you have them, as they give you exactly the amount you need.

Sweethearts

To make about 30 sweethearts, you will need:

¾ cup powdered sugar
¼ cup super-fine granulated sugar
1 cup finely-crushed almonds*
¼ cup full-fat sweetened condensed milk
red food coloring
one medium and one small heart-shaped cookie cutter
a baking sheet covered with wax paper

These candies need to be eaten within four days.

1. Sift the powdered sugar into a large bowl. Add the sugar and almonds and stir them all together.

2. Make a hollow in the middle and add the condensed milk. Mix it in well, until the mixture is completely smooth.

3. Put half of the mixture into another bowl. Add two drops of red food coloring. Mix it in really well, using your fingers.

4. Wrap both pieces of mixture in foodwrap. Put them in a refrigerator for 20 minutes. This makes them easier to roll out.

5. Sprinkle powdered sugar onto a clean work surface. Roll out the pink piece, until it is about as thick as your little finger.

6. Use the larger cutter to cut out heart shapes. Cut them close together. Make the scraps into a ball, and roll it out.

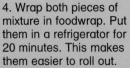

* Don't give these to anyone who is allergic to nuts.

7. Cut out more hearts.
Then, use the smaller
cutter to cut out hearts
from the middles of the
big hearts.

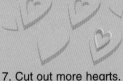

8. Roll out the cream
mixture, as before. Cut
out large hearts. Then,
cut small hearts out of
their middles.

9. Gently press the small
cream hearts into the big
pink ones. Then, press
the small pink hearts
into the big cream ones.

10. Put the hearts onto
the baking sheet. Leave
them to dry and harden
overnight. Store them in
an airtight box.

Tropical fruit cups

To make 12 tropical fruit cups, you will need:

2oz. sweetened dried pineapple or mango
1 tablespoon pineapple or orange juice
½ cup milk chocolate or semi-sweet
    chocolate chips
½ cup white chocolate chips
    small foil or double thickness paper cups
    for candy

*These chocolates need to be
eaten within five days.*

1. Put the pineapple or mango onto a cutting board. Using a sharp knife, carefully cut the fruit into tiny pieces.

2. Put about a quarter of the chopped fruit on one side. Put the rest into a small bowl, and add the fruit juice. Stir it well.

3. Cover the bowl with plastic foodwrap. Leave the fruit for half an hour or until it has soaked up the juice.

*Do this while the
fruit is soaking.*

*Wear oven
gloves when you
lift the bowl out.*

4. Fill a pan with about 1 in. of water. Heat the pan until the water bubbles, then remove it from the heat.

5. Put the chocolate chips into a heatproof bowl. Wearing oven gloves, carefully put the bowl into the pan.

6. Stir the chocolate with a wooden spoon until it has melted. Lift the bowl out of the pan. Leave it to cool for three minutes.

Spread the chocolate all the way up the sides.

7. Spread chocolate over the inside of the candy cups with a teaspoon. Put them in a refrigerator for 20 minutes, until firm.

8. Spoon some of the soaked fruit into each chocolate cup. Each cup should be just over half full.

9. Melt the white chocolate in the same way that you melted the milk chocolate. Leave it to cool for three minutes.

10. Spoon the white chocolate over the fruit, so that it comes right to the top of the milk chocolate cups.

11. Put a piece of fruit on each chocolate. Chill them in a refrigerator for half an hour. Then, peel off the paper cups.

12. Put the chocolates in an airtight container. Keep them in a refrigerator until you are ready to eat them.

Creamy coconut ice

To make 36 squares, you will need:

2 egg whites, mixed from dried or pasteurized
liquid egg white (as directed on package)
1lb. box powdered sugar, sifted
2 cups finely shredded coconut (sweetened)
3 teaspoons water
2 drops green food coloring
a shallow 8in. cake pan
a piece of wax paper

Coconut ice needs to be eaten within 10 days.

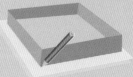 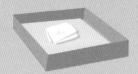

1. Put the pan onto a piece of wax paper. Draw around it and cut out the square, just inside the line.

2. Use a paper towel to wipe some oil onto the sides and bottom of the pan. Press in the paper square and wipe it too.

3. Put the egg whites into a large bowl. Stir them quickly with a fork for about a minute, until they are frothy.

To make pink and white coconut ice, use red food coloring instead of green.

4. Stir in two tablespoons of powdered sugar. Add and stir in the rest of the sugar, a little at a time, until it is all mixed in.

5. Add the coconut and water and mix everything well. Spoon half of the mixture into the pan. Use your fingers to press it in.

6. Add a few drops of green food coloring to the rest of the mixture. Stir the mixture until it is evenly colored.

Smooth the top with the back of a spoon.

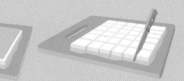

7. Spoon the green mixture on top of the white layer. Then, leave the pan in a cool place overnight.

8. Use a blunt knife to loosen the edges of the coconut ice. Turn it out onto a cutting board. Then, remove the paper.

9. Cut the coconut ice into 36 small squares. Leave them to harden for two hours. Keep them in an airtight container.

Chocolate truffles

To make about 15 truffles, you will need:

1 cup semi-sweet or milk chocolate chips
2 tablespoons butter
¼ cup powdered sugar
¼ cup crushed vanilla wafers
½ cup chocolate sprinkles
paper miniature candy cups

Chocolate truffles need to be eaten
within five days.

Put chocolate truffles in boxes
lined with tissue paper, to
give as presents.

1. Fill a pan with about 1 in. of water. Heat the pan until the water bubbles, then remove it from the heat.

2. Put the chocolate chips and butter into a heatproof bowl. Wearing oven gloves, gently put the bowl into the pan.

Wear oven gloves when you lift the bowl out.

3. Stir the chocolate and butter with a wooden spoon until they have melted. Carefully lift the bowl out of the water.

4. Sift the powdered sugar into the chocolate. Add the cookie crumbs and stir until everything is mixed well.

5. Leave the chocolate mixture to cool in the bowl. Then, put the chocolate sprinkles onto a plate.

Use a teaspoon.

6. When the mixture is firm and thick, scoop up some with a teaspoon and put it into the chocolate sprinkles.

Roll the spoonful to make a ball.

7. Using your fingers, roll the spoonful around until it is covered. Then, put it in a paper cup. Make lots more truffles.

8. Put them onto a plate. Put them in a refrigerator for 30 minutes. Keep them in the refrigerator in an airtight container.

Chocolate-dipped fruit

You will need:

16oz. (1 lb.) small strawberries
 with their stems left on
½ cup milk chocolate chips
½ cup white chocolate chips
a piece of wax paper

*The chocolate-dipped fruit needs to
be eaten on the day you make it.*

*You can also dip other kinds of
fruit in chocolate. Mandarin
orange segments look pretty
and taste delicious.*

1. Put the strawberries in a sieve. Wash them under cold running water for a little time, to rinse them.

2. Gently pat them with a paper towel to remove most of the water. Then, spread them out on a plate. Leave them to dry.

3. Fill a pan with about 1 in. of water. Heat the pan until the water bubbles, then remove it from the heat.

4. Put the chocolate chips into a heatproof bowl. Wearing oven gloves, carefully put the bowl into the pan.

5. Use a wooden spoon to stir the chocolate until it has melted. Using oven gloves, carefully lift the bowl out of the water.

6. Melt the white chocolate chips in the same way. Leave both bowls of chocolate to cool for two minutes.

7. Dip a strawberry into one of the bowls of chocolate. The chocolate should come about half-way up the strawberry.

8. Lift the strawberry out and let it drip over the bowl. Then, put it on a piece of wax paper on a plate.

9. Dip the other strawberries into the chocolate. Put them in the refrigerator for about 20 minutes, to set.

10. Carefully peel the strawberries off the wax paper, and put them on a plate. Eat them on the same day.

Mini florentines

To make about 18 mini florentines, you will need:

18 Maraschino cherries
18 unsalted mixed whole nuts, such as halved walnuts
  or pecans*
½ cup semi-sweet or milk chocolate chips
½ cup white chocolate chips
a baking sheet covered with wax paper

Mini florentines
need to be eaten
within four days.

These mini
florentines are
topped with
pecan nuts
and cherries.

1: Put the cherries in a sieve. Rinse them under warm running water to remove the syrup. Dry them on a paper towel.

2. Put the cherries onto a cutting board. Chop each one carefully, using a sharp knife. Then, chop the nuts too.

3. Fill a pan with about 1 in. of water. Heat the pan until the water bubbles, then remove it from the heat.

* Don't give these to anyone who is allergic to nuts.

4. Put the chocolate chips into a heatproof bowl. Wearing oven gloves, carefully put the bowl into the pan.

5. Stir the chocolate with a wooden spoon until it has melted. Using oven gloves, carefully lift the bowl out of the pan.

6. Spoon a teaspoon of melted chocolate onto the wax paper. Make a neat circle, using the back of the spoon.

7. Gently press pieces of cherry and nut into the chocolate. Make more circles of chocolate and decorate them.

8. Then, melt the white chocolate chips. Make more circles with the chocolate and decorate them too.

9. Put the florentines in the refrigerator for half an hour. Carefully peel them off the paper. Keep them in an airtight container.

Chocolate swirls

To make about 25 chocolate swirls, you will need:

2¼ cups powdered sugar
half the white of a medium egg, mixed from dried or
    pasteurized liquid egg white (as directed on package)
1 teaspoon lemon juice
¼ teaspoon mint extract
1 tablespoon cocoa powder
2 teaspoons boiling water
½ teaspoon vanilla
a baking sheet covered in plastic foodwrap

Eat these within 10 days.

Pour the mixture into the hollow in the powdered sugar.

1. Sift the powdered sugar then put 1 cup of it into a large bowl. Make a hollow in the middle with a spoon.

2. Mix half of the egg white, the lemon juice and mint extract in a small bowl. Pour the mixture into the powdered sugar.

3. Stir the mixture with a blunt knife, then squeeze it with your fingers until it is smooth. Wrap it in plastic foodwrap.

4. Sift the cocoa powder into a large bowl. Add the water and vanilla. Then, mix everything together well.

5. Add the rest of the egg white and stir it in. Add 1 cup of the powdered sugar. Then, stir the mixture with a blunt knife.

If the mixture is a little dry, add a drop of water.

6. Squeeze the mixture until it is smooth. Wrap it in foodwrap. Put both pieces in a refrigerator for 10 minutes.

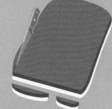

7. Sprinkle a little of the powdered sugar onto a clean work surface and a rolling pin. This keeps the mixture from sticking.

8. Roll out the white piece of mixture into a rectangle 6 in. by 8 in. Then, do the same with the chocolate mixture.

9. Put the chocolate rectangle on top of the white one. Then, trim the edges with a knife to make them straight.

Roll the rectangle from one of the long edges.

10. Tightly roll the rectangle into a sausage. Wrap it in foodwrap and put it in a refrigerator for about 10 minutes.

11. Using a sharp knife, carefully cut the sausage into slices which are about the thickness of your little finger.

12. Put the swirls onto the baking sheet. Leave them to harden overnight. Keep them in an airtight container.

Chocolate bugs

To make 10 bugs, you will need:

½ cup semi-sweet or milk chocolate chips
3 tablespoons corn syrup
½ cup white chocolate chips

The bugs need
to be eaten
within a week.

Use a wooden spoon.

1. Fill a pan with about 1 in. of water. Heat the pan until the water bubbles, then remove the pan from the heat.

2. Put the chocolate chips into a heatproof bowl. Using oven gloves, carefully put the bowl into the pan.

3. Stir the chocolate until it has melted. Wearing oven gloves, lift the bowl out of the pan. Leave it to cool for two minutes.

4. Stir in 1½ tablespoons of corn syrup until the mixture forms a thick paste which doesn't stick to the sides of the bowl.

5. Wrap the paste in plastic foodwrap. Then, melt the white chocolate and stir in the rest of the corn syrup, as before.

6. Wrap the white paste in plastic foodwrap. Chill both pieces of chocolate paste in the refrigerator for about an hour.

You could also decorate the bugs with stripes or wiggly lines.

7. Take both pieces of chocolate paste out of the refrigerator. Leave them for about 10 minutes, to soften a little.

8. Cut the chocolate paste into six pieces. Wrap one piece in foodwrap again and put it on one side.

Smooth the edges of the oval shapes.

9. Make the other five pieces into oval shapes. Do the same with the white chocolate paste, to make 10 ovals altogether.

Make a shallow mark with the knife.

10. To make a bug's head, gently press in the back of a blunt knife, a third of the way down a chocolate shape.

The second mark makes the wings.

11. Make a second mark. Unwrap the last pieces of paste. Roll small balls to make eyes and spots. Press them onto the bug.

12. Put the bugs onto a plate. Cover them with plastic foodwrap. Keep them in the refrigerator until you eat them.

Marshmallow crunch

To make about 50 squares, you will need:

1oz. (about 8) candied cherries
2 cups puffed rice cereal
1½ cups miniature marshmallows
2 tablespoons butter
a shallow 8in. cake pan
a piece of wax paper

*Marshmallow crunch needs
to be eaten within three days.*

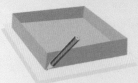

1. Put the pan onto a piece of wax paper. Draw around it and cut out the square, just inside the line.

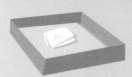

2. Use a paper towel to wipe some oil onto the sides and bottom of the pan. Press in the paper square and wipe it too.

3. Put the cherries onto a cutting board. Carefully cut them into small pieces, using a sharp knife.

4. Put the puffed rice cereal and chopped cherries into a bowl. Mix them well with a wooden spoon.

5. Put the miniature marshmallows into a large pan. Then, add the butter, and mix everything together.

6. Gently heat the pan, stirring occasionally with a wooden spoon. Continue until everything has just melted.

Use a wooden spoon.

7. Remove the pan from the heat. Add the cereal mixture to the pan and stir everything until it is mixed together.

Push the mixture into the corners and smooth it down.

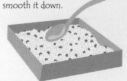

8. Spoon the mixture into the pan, and put it in the refrigerator for two hours. Then, loosen the edges with a blunt knife.

9. Turn the crunch out onto a board. Remove the paper. Cut the crunch into squares. Keep it in an airtight container.

Creamy fondants

To make about 15-20 creamy fondants, you will need:

2 cups powdered sugar
half the white of a small egg, mixed from dried egg
   white (as directed on package)
½ teaspoon vanilla
4 teaspoons light cream
red and green food coloring
small cookie cutters
a cookie sheet covered
   in plastic foodwrap

These candies need to be eaten within a week.

This helps to stop the mixture from sticking.

1. Sift the powdered sugar into a large bowl. Make a hole in the middle of the sugar with a spoon.

2. Mix the egg white, vanilla and light cream in a small bowl. Pour the mixture into the powdered sugar.

3. Use a blunt knife to stir the mixture. Squeeze it between your fingers until it is smooth. Then, cut it into two halves.

4. Put each half into a separate bowl. Add a few drops of red food coloring to one bowl, and green coloring to the other.

5. Mix in the red coloring with your fingers. Add more sugar if the mixture is sticky. Mix the green coloring in the other bowl.

6. Sprinkle a little powdered sugar onto a clean work surface. Sprinkle some onto a rolling pin too.

Put creamy
fondants in boxes,
to give as
presents.

Cut the shapes
close together.

7. Roll out the pink
mixture until it is about
as thick as your little
finger. Use cutters to cut
out lots of shapes.

8. Use a blunt knife to
lift the shapes onto a
cookie sheet. Roll out
the green mixture and
cut out more shapes.

9. Put the shapes onto
the cookie sheet. Leave
for an hour to harden.
Keep them in an airtight
container in a refrigerator.

Orange and lemon creams

To make about 24 orange and lemon creams, you will need:

3½ cups powdered sugar
1 orange (small)
half the white of a small egg, mixed from dried or pasteurized liquid egg white (as directed on package)
red and yellow food coloring
1 lemon
a baking sheet covered with wax paper

These candies need to be eaten within 10 days.

Gift bags filled with orange and lemon creams make great gifts. Find out how to make them on page 32.

Use the small holes on a grater.

Use a lemon squeezer.

1. Sift the powdered sugar. Put half of it into one bowl and half into another. Grate about half of the skin of the orange.

2. Cut the orange in half and squeeze. Put the juice into a bowl. Then, put 1½ teaspoons of egg white into another bowl.

3. Add the grated orange, 5 teaspoons of juice, a drop of red food coloring and two drops of yellow. Mix everything well.

Add more powdered sugar if it's too moist.

The marks make the outsides look like orange skin.

4. Add the mixture to one of the bowls of powdered sugar. Stir it with a blunt knife, then squeeze it with your fingers.

5. Sprinkle powdered sugar on a clean work surface. Make 12 orange balls. Then, gently roll them over a fine grater.

6. Grate about half of the lemon's skin. Cut the lemon in half. Squeeze it and put 5 teaspoons of the juice into a bowl.

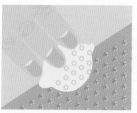

7. Add a few drops of yellow food coloring, the grated lemon and 1½ teaspoons of egg white. Mix everything together.

8. Mix the juice mixture into the other bowl of powdered sugar. Make 12 lemon shapes. Roll them over a fine grater.

9. Put the candy onto the baking sheet. Leave them for a few hours to become firm. Keep them in an airtight container.

White marshmallow fudge

To make 36 pieces, you will need:

1lb. box powdered sugar, preferably unrefined
4oz. (about 16) jumbo-sized white marshmallows
2 tablespoons milk
1 stick (½ cup) unsalted butter
½ teaspoon vanilla
a shallow 8in. cake pan
a piece of wax paper

The fudge needs to be eaten within a week.

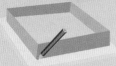

1. Put the pan onto a piece of wax paper. Draw around it and cut out the square, just inside the line.

2. Use a paper towel to wipe some oil onto the sides and bottom of the pan. Press in the paper square and wipe it too.

3. Sift the powdered sugar into a large bowl. Make a small hollow in the middle of the powdered sugar.

4. Using scissors, cut the marshmallows in half and put them into a small pan. Add the milk, butter and vanilla.

5. Gently heat the mixture. Stir it every now and then with a wooden spoon until everything has melted.

6. Pour the mixture into the hollow in the powdered sugar. Beat everything together with a spoon until it is smooth

Smooth the fudge with the back of a spoon.

7. Put the fudge into the pan and push it into the corners. Use a spoon to make the top of the fudge as flat as you can.

Find out how to wrap pieces of fudge like this on page 31.

8. When the fudge is cool, put the pan in a refrigerator for about three hours, or until the fudge is firm.

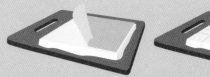

9. Use a blunt knife to loosen the edges of the fudge, then turn it out onto a cutting board. Remove the paper.

10. Cut the fudge into 36 pieces. Then, put it in a refrigerator for an hour to harden. Keep it in an airtight container.

Chocolate and apricot drops

To make about 25 chocolate and apricot drops, you will need:

1¼ cups animal cookies (crumbled)
2oz. (14 halves) dried apricots
1⅓ cups white chocolate chips
4 tablespoons corn syrup
1 teaspoon hot cocoa mix
small paper cups for candy

These chocolates need to be eaten within three days.

1. Break the cookies into tiny pieces and put them into a bowl. Cut the apricots into tiny pieces. Add them to the cookies.

2. Fill a pan with about 1 in. of water. Heat the pan until the water bubbles, then remove it from the heat.

Wear oven gloves when you lift the bowl out.

3. Put the white chocolate chips into a heatproof bowl. Wearing oven gloves, carefully put the bowl into the pan.

4. Stir the chocolate until it has melted. Carefully lift the bowl out of the water. Let the chocolate cool for a minute.

You can also make these chocolates with semi-sweet or milk chocolate, and dust them with powdered sugar.

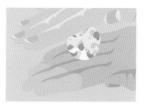

5. Quickly stir in the corn syrup, then add the cookies and apricots. Mix everything well with a wooden spoon.

6. Scoop up some of the mixture with a teaspoon. Using your hands, shape it into a ball and put it into a paper cup.

7. Make more balls and put them onto a large plate. Put them in the refrigerator for an hour, until they are firm.

8. Sift the cocoa mix over the chocolate and apricot drops. Keep them in an airtight container in the refrigerator.

Wrapping ideas

Gift bags

1. Cut a square of thin cellophane. Then, lay five or six pieces of candy in the middle of the square.

2. Gather up the edges of the square around the candy. Then, pull the edges together above the candy, like this.

3. Cut a piece of ribbon about 8 inches long. Tie the ribbon tightly around the bag, above the candy.

Pointed bags

The white line shows you where to cut.

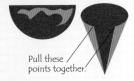

Pull these points together.

1. Cut a square of cellophane with sides 16 inches long. Fold it in half, and then in half again.

2. Hold the corner where the folds join. Cut a quarter-circle, like this. Open out the cellophane shape. It is now a circle.

3. Cut the circle in half. Take one of the halves. Then, pull its two points toward each other until they meet.

4. Slide one of the points behind the other, to make a cone. Secure the cone with pieces of tape.

5. Half-fill the cone with candy. Cut a piece of ribbon 8 inches long. Tie it around the cone, above the candy.

Line a gift box with cellophane, then fill it with layers of candy.

Wrapped candy

Find out how to make sparkling gift tags on page 32.

Use a tiny piece of tape.

1. Cut a square of thin cellophane that is bigger than the candy. Put the candy in the middle of the square.

2. Wrap the candy in the piece of cellophane and tape it. Tie pieces of ribbon around each end of the candy.

Sparkling gift tags

Ask someone to help you cut the potato.

1. Carefully cut a potato in half. Press the sharp edge of a star-shaped cookie cutter into the cut side of the potato.

2. Press the edge of the star cutter into some household glue. Press the cutter onto a piece of thin cardboard.

3. Before the glue dries, sprinkle it with lots of glitter. Shake off any extra glitter onto some scrap paper.

4. Cut around the star, a little way away from the glitter. Tape a piece of ribbon to the back of the tag.

YUMMY THINGS FOR CHRISTMAS

Little Christmas trees

To make 10 trees and 16 presents, you will need:

2 cups self-rising flour
1 cup soft margarine
4 tablespoons of milk
1 level teaspoon of baking powder
1 cup sugar
2-3 drops vanilla
4 medium eggs

For the butter icing:
2/3 cup butter, softened
2½ cups powdered sugar
1 teaspoon of vanilla
food dyes

Preheat the oven to 350°F.

You could arrange the presents around the trees.

Use a 13 x 9 inch baking pan.

Use a paper towel to wipe oil on the pan.

Use a wooden spoon.

1. Draw around a pan on greaseproof paper. Cut it out. Wipe oil inside the pan. Put the paper into the pan, and grease it.

2. Sift the flour into a large mixing bowl. Add the margarine, milk, baking powder, sugar and vanilla.

3. Break the eggs into a small bowl. Beat them with a fork. Add them to the flour mixture. Beat everything together well.

Make trunks for the trees from chocolate bars or cookies.

The cake should be springy when you press it. Be careful, as it will be hot.

4. Spoon the mixture into the pan. Smooth the top. Bake it in the oven for 40-45 minutes, until the middle is springy.

5. Leave the cake in the pan to cool, then lift it out. Put the butter into a bowl. Beat it with a wooden spoon until it is creamy.

6. Sift in the powdered sugar. Stir it in, a little at a time. Stir in the vanilla. Put three-quarters of the icing in a bowl.

To make the color stronger, add more dye, a drop at a time.

7. Mix in a little green food dye. Divide the rest of the icing into three bowls. Mix a drop of food dye into each one.

—These will be the presents.

8. Cut a strip 3in. wide from one end of the cake. Cut it into 16 small squares. Cut the cake in half along its length.

9. Cut out ten triangles. Ice them with green icing. Ice the presents with the colored icing. Press candy onto the cakes.

Decorate the trees with candy.

Coconut mice

To make about eight large mice, five medium
mice and three baby mice, you will need:
2 cups powdered sugar, sifted
1 cup condensed milk
3 cups shredded coconut
red food dye
candy for ears
red licorice strings

1. Mix the powdered
sugar and the condensed
milk in a bowl. Mix in the
coconut. Put the mixture
into two bowls.

2. Add a few drops of
red dye to each bowl
and mix it in. Then add a
few more drops of dye to
one of the bowls.

*For baby mice,
use a teaspoon
for the body.*

3. Dip a clean tablespoon into some water and let it drip. Then, lift out a big spoonful of the mixture.

4. Pat the spoonful smooth on top. Turn the spoon over and put the shape onto a piece of plastic foodwrap.

5. Pinch a nose at the thinner end of the spoon shape. Then, add candy for the mouse's ears and eyes.

6. Push some licorice under the shape, as a tail. Leave the mouse to harden on a plate. Make more mice.

Use a small spoon for a medium mouse.

Spicy Christmas stars

To make about 25 stars, you will need:
1¼ cups self-rising flour
½ teaspoon of mild paprika
½ teaspoon salt
⅓ cup margarine
⅔ cup cheese, finely grated
1 egg and 2 tablespoons of milk, beaten together
star-shaped cutter
greased cookie sheet

Preheat the oven to 400°F.

1. Sift the flour, paprika and salt into a bowl. Add the margarine and rub it with your fingers to make fine crumbs.

2. Leave a tablespoon of the grated cheese on a saucer. Add the rest of the cheese to the bowl and stir it in.

3. Put a tablespoon of the beaten egg and milk mixture into a cup. Mix the rest into the flour to make a dough.

Use a rolling pin.

Use a pastry brush.

4. Sprinkle flour onto a clean work surface. Roll out the dough, until it is slightly thinner than your little finger.

5. Use the cutter to cut out star shapes. Cut them close together. Make the scraps into a ball, and roll them out.

6. Cut out more stars. Brush the stars with the rest of the egg mixture, then sprinkle them with the rest of the cheese.

7. Put the stars onto the greased cookie sheet. Bake them in the oven for eight to ten minutes, until they are golden.

These stars are delicious to eat when they are warm.

Creamy chocolate fudge

To make about 36 squares of fudge, you will need:
½ cup full-fat cream cheese
1 level tablespoon cocoa powder
2 cups powdered sugar
1 teaspoon of cooking oil, for greasing
½ cup semi-sweet chocolate chips
2 tablespoons butter
a shallow square cake or brownie pan
greaseproof paper

Find out how to wrap pieces of fudge on page 62.

Use a pencil to draw around the pan.

1. Put the cream cheese into a bowl. Sift the cocoa and powdered sugar into the bowl too. Mix them together well.

2. Put the cake pan onto a sheet of greaseproof paper and draw around it. Cut out the shape, just inside the line.

3. Use a paper towel to wipe oil onto the sides and base of the pan. Press in the paper square and wipe it too.

4. Melt the chocolate and butter as in steps 1-3 on page 9. Then, stir in a tablespoon of the cream cheese mixture.

5. Pour the chocolate into the cheese mixture in the bowl. Beat them together with a spoon until they are creamy.

6. Spoon the mixture into the pan, and push it into the corners. Make the top of the fudge as flat as you can.

7. Smooth the top with the back of a spoon. Put the pan in the refrigerator for two hours, or until the fudge is firm.

8. Use a blunt knife to loosen the edges of the fudge, then turn it out onto a large plate. Remove the paper.

9. Cut the fudge into lots of squares. Then, put the plate in the refrigerator for two hours, until the fudge is hard.

Crinkly Christmas pies

To make 12 pies, you will need:
4 apples
3 tablespoons orange juice or cold water
½ cup dried cranberries or raisins
2 teaspoons sugar
½ teaspoon ground cinnamon
14oz filo dough (about 6 sheets)
2 tablespoons butter
2 tablespoons powdered sugar
twelve hole muffin tin

Preheat the oven to 375°F.

You may need to ask someone to help you.

1. Peel the apples. Cut them into quarters and cut out the cores. Cut them into small pieces and put them in the pan.

Put the lid back on after you've stirred the apples.

2. Add the juice or water and put the pan on very low heat. Cover it with a lid. Cook for 20 minutes, stirring often.

Stir the mixture often.

3. Stir in the fruit, sugar and cinnamon. Cook the mixture for about five minutes, then take it off the heat.

Keep the six sheets together.

4. Take the pan off the heat. Unwrap the dough. Cut all the sheets into six squares. Cover them with foodwrap.

Use a pastry brush.

5. Put the butter in a small pan and melt it over a low heat. Brush a little butter over one of the dough squares.

6. Put the square into a hole in the tray, buttered side up. Press it gently into the hole. Brush butter onto another square.

Overlap the dough sheets so that they look like a star.

7. Put this square over the first one. Overlap the corners slightly. Butter and add a third square. Repeat in all the holes.

8. Put the tray on the middle shelf of the oven and cook for 10 minutes. Take it out and leave it to cool for five minutes.

Heat the apples until they bubble a little.

9. Take the pastry cases out of the tray and put them onto a large plate. Heat the apples again for about two minutes.

Eat the pies warm or cold.

10. Spoon the apple mixture into the pastry cases, so that they are almost full. Sift powdered sugar onto them.

Painted cookies

To make about 15 cookies, you will need:
½ cup powdered sugar
½ cup soft margarine
the yolk from a large egg
vanilla
1¼ cups flour
plastic foodwrap
big cookie cutters
greased cookie sheet

To decorate the cookies:
an egg yolk
food dyes

Preheat the oven to 350°F.

Use a wooden spoon.

1. Sift the powdered sugar through a sieve into a large bowl. Add the margarine. Mix well until they are smooth.

2. Add the large egg yolk and stir it in well. Then, add a few drops of vanilla extract. Stir the vanilla into the mixture.

3. Hold a sieve over the bowl and pour the flour into it. Sift the flour through the sieve, to remove any lumps.

4. Mix in the flour until you get a smooth dough. Wrap the dough in plastic foodwrap and put it in the freezer.

Decorate your cookies with lots of different patterns.

It takes time to decorate the cookies, so you could freeze some of the dough to use another day.

5. Put the egg yolk into a bowl and beat it with a fork. Put it onto saucers. Mix a few drops of food dye into each one.

6. Take the dough out of the freezer. Roll out half of it onto a floury work surface, until it is as thin as your little finger.

7. Press out shapes with cutters. Use a spatula to lift them onto a cookie sheet. Roll out the rest of the dough.

8. Cut out more shapes. Use a clean paintbrush to paint shapes on the cookies with the egg and dye mixture.

9. Bake the cookies for 10-12 minutes. Remove them from the oven. Let them cool a little, then lift them onto a wire rack.

Starry jam tart

To make one jam tart, you will need:
12oz ready-made pie-crust
about 2 tablespoons flour
6 rounded tablespoons seedless raspberry or
strawberry preserves
1 tablespoon milk
1 shallow pie tin
small star-shaped cutter

Preheat the oven to 400°F.

You can use any
shape of cutter you
like. Stars and holly
leaves look very
Christmassy.

1. Take the dough out of the refrigerator and leave it for 10 minutes. Sprinkle a clean work surface with some flour.

2. Cut off a quarter of the dough and wrap it in some plastic foodwrap. Sprinkle some flour onto a rolling pin.

Sift a slice of tart with a little powdered sugar and serve it with whipped cream or ice cream.

The rolling pin cuts off the extra dough.

3. Roll out the bigger piece of dough. Turn it a little, then roll it again. Make a circle about 12in. across.

4. Put the rolling pin at one side of the dough. Roll the dough around it and lift it up. Place it over the tin and unroll it.

5. Dip a finger into some flour and press the dough into the edges of the tin. Then, roll the rolling pin across the top.

6. Spoon the preserves into the dough crust. Spread it out with the back of a spoon. Roll out the rest of the dough.

7. Using the cutter, cut out about 12 shapes. Brush them with a little milk and place them on top of the preserves.

The pastry should be golden brown.

8. Put the jam tart in the oven. Bake it for about 20 minutes. Take the tart from the oven and let the jam cool before serving.

Peppermint creams

To make about 25 peppermint creams, you will need:
2 cups powdered sugar
half the white of a small egg mixed from powdered egg
or powdered meringue
(mix as directed on container)
¼ teaspoon peppermint flavoring
1 tablespoon lemon juice
green food dye
rolling pin
small cutters
a cookie sheet covered in
plastic foodwrap

Put peppermint creams in boxes, to give as presents.

1. Sift the powdered sugar through a sieve into a large bowl. Make a hole in the middle of the sugar with a spoon.

2. Mix the egg white, peppermint flavoring and lemon juice in a small bowl. Pour the mixture into the sugar.

3. Use a blunt knife to stir the mixture. Then, squeeze it between your fingers until it is smooth, like a dough.

The powdered sugar stops the mixture from sticking.

4. Cut the mixture into two pieces. Put each piece into a bowl. Add a few drops of green food dye to one bowl.

5. Use your fingers to mix in the dye. If the mixture is sticky, add a little more powdered sugar and mix it in.

6. Sprinkle a little powdered sugar onto a clean work surface. Sprinkle some onto a rolling pin too.

Cut the
shapes close
together.

7. Roll out the green
mixture until it is about
as thick as your little
finger. Use cutters to cut
out lots of shapes.

8. Use a blunt knife to
lift the shapes onto the
cookie sheet. Roll out
the white mixture and
cut out more shapes.

9. Lift all the shapes
onto the cookie sheet.
Leave them for at least
an hour until they
become hard.

Shortbread

To make eight pieces, you will need:
butter for greasing
1½ cups flour
½ cup butter, refrigerated, cut into chunks
¼ cup sugar
an 8-inch shallow pan

Preheat the oven to 300°F.

1. Grease the bottom and sides of the pan with some butter on a piece of paper towel. Make sure it is all greased.

2. Sift the flour through a sieve into a large bowl. Then, add the chunks of butter to the bowl too.

3. Mix in the butter so that it is coated in flour. Rub it into the flour with your fingers until it is like fine breadcrumbs.

4. Stir in the sugar with a wooden spoon. Hold the bowl with one hand and squeeze the mixture into a ball with the other.

5. Press the mixture into the pan with your fingers. Use the back of a spoon to smooth the top and make it level.

6. Use a fork to press patterns around the edge and holes in the middle. Cut the shortbread into eight pieces.

*Shortbread makes an ideal present.
See pages 62-63 for wrapping ideas.*

7. Bake the shortbread for 30 minutes, until it is golden. After 10 minutes, take it out of the pan. Put it on a wire rack to cool.

Party muffins

To make 10 muffins, you will need:

2½ cups all-purpose flour
2 teaspoons baking powder
¾ cup granulated sugar
1 lemon
4 tablespoons butter
1 cup milk
1 medium egg
½ cup (4oz) seedless raspberry preserves
a 12-hole muffin tray
small candies and sugar strands, for decorating

For the icing:
1½ cups powdered sugar
2 tablespoons lemon juice squeezed from the lemon from the main mixture

Preheat your oven to 400°F.

✿ The muffins need to be stored in an airtight container and should be eaten on the day you make them.

Use a pastry brush.

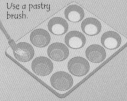

If you are having a party, you could decorate some of the muffins with little candles.

1. Brush oil in ten of the muffin holes. Then, cut a small circle of baking parchment to put in the bottom of each hole.

2. Sift flour and baking powder into a large bowl. Add granulated sugar, then mix everything with a metal spoon.

Use a lemon squeezer.

3. Grate rind from the lemon using the medium holes on a grater. Then, cut the lemon in half and squeeze the juice from it.

4. Put two tablespoons of juice on one side, for the icing. Then, cut the butter into pieces and put it in a pan with the lemon rind.

5. Add four tablespoons of milk and heat the pan until the butter melts. Take it off the heat and add the rest of the milk.

6. Break the egg into a cup and mix it well with a fork, then stir it into the butter mixture. Add the mixture to the bowl.

7. Stir everything together with a fork. Nearly fill each muffin hole with the mixture and bake the muffins for 15 minutes.

8. Leave the muffins in the tray for three minutes, then loosen them with a blunt knife. Put them on a wire rack to cool.

Use a sharp knife.

9. Turn each muffin on its side and cut it in half. Then, spread preserves on the bottom half and lay the top half on top.

10. Sift powdered sugar into a bowl and mix in lemon juice. Spoon icing onto the muffins and press on some candies.

Shining star cookies

To make about 20 cookies, you will need:
½ cup soft brown sugar
⅓ cup soft margarine
half a small egg
1¼ cups flour
1 teaspoon allspice
hard candy, assorted flavors
large star-shaped cookie cutter
fat drinking straw
small round cookie cutter,
slightly bigger than the candy
large cookie sheet lined with baking parchment

Preheat the oven to 350°F.

Thread thin ribbon through the holes.

1. Using a wooden spoon, mix the brown sugar and margarine really well, getting rid of any lumps in the mixture.

2. Break the egg into a separate bowl. Beat the egg with a fork until the yolk and the white are mixed together.

3. Mix half of the beaten egg into the mixture in the bowl, a little at a time. You don't need the other half.

4. Sift the flour and allspice through a sieve. Mix everything together really well with a wooden spoon.

5. Squeeze the mixture with your hands until a firm dough is formed. Make the dough into a large ball.

6. Sprinkle a clean work surface with a little flour. Then, roll out the ball of dough until it is ¼ of an inch thick.

If you hang cookies on a Christmas tree, don't eat them afterward.

7. Line the cookie sheet. Use a large cutter to press out lots of stars. Use a spatula to put them onto the sheet.

8. Make a hole in each star by pressing the straw through the dough, near the top of one of the points.

9. Use a small cookie cutter to cut a hole in the middle of each star. The hole should be slightly bigger than the candy.

10. Squeeze the leftover pieces of dough into a ball. Roll them out. Cut out more stars. Put them on the cookie sheet.

11. Drop a piece of candy into the hole in the middle of each star. Put the cookie sheet on the middle shelf of the oven.

12. Bake the shapes for twelve minutes, then take them out. Leave them on the cookie sheet until they are cold.

Snowmen and presents

To make lots of snowmen
and presents, you will need:
9oz 'white' marzipan*
green, red and yellow
food dyes
toothpicks

Coloring marzipan

Add a little powdered
sugar if the marzipan
gets too sticky.

1. Unwrap the marzipan.
Then, put it on a plate
and cut it into quarters.
Put each quarter into a
small bowl.

2. Add one drop of green
food dye. Mix it in with
your fingers. Continue
until the marzipan is
evenly colored.

3. Leave one quarter of
the marzipan 'white'.
Add red food dye to one
quarter, and yellow to
the other. Mix in the dye.

A snowman

Put the marzipan
balls on a plate.

Press the ball
with your
thumb.

Cross the
ends of the
scarf.

1. Roll a piece of 'white'
marzipan into a ball.
Then, make a smaller
ball. Press the smaller
ball onto the larger one.

2. Roll a small ball of red
marzipan. Press it to
make a circle. Put it on
the snowman's head. Put
a tiny red ball on top.

3. Roll a thin strip of
red marzipan. Wrap it
around the snowman for
a scarf. Press in a face
with a toothpick.

* Marzipan contains ground nuts. Don't make these if you are allergic to nuts.

Ice a cake with butter icing (see pages 34-35) and decorate it with snowmen and presents.

A present

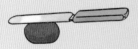

1. Roll a ball of red marzipan and put it on a work surface. Gently press the flat side of a knife down on the ball.

2. Turn the ball on its side and press it with the knife again. Keep on doing this until the ball becomes a cube.

3. Roll thin strips of green marzipan. Press them onto the cube, in a cross. Add two loops in the middle for a bow.

Iced gingerbread hearts

To make about 20 cookies, you will need:
2 cups flour
2 teaspoons of ground ginger
2 teaspoons of baking soda
½ cup butter or margarine, cut into chunks
¾ cup soft light brown sugar
¾ cup white sugar
1 medium egg
4 tablespoons of maple syrup
white writing icing
large heart-shaped cookie cutter
2 greased cookie sheets

Preheat the oven to 375°F.

You could wrap some cookies in tissue paper or cellophane twists, to give as a present.

1. Sift the flour, ground ginger and baking soda into a large bowl. Then, add the butter or margarine chunks.

2. Rub the butter or margarine into the flour with your fingers until it is like fine breadcrumbs. Stir in the sugar.

3. Break the egg into a small bowl, then add the syrup. Beat well with a fork, then stir the egg mixture into the flour.

4. Mix with a metal spoon until you make a dough. Sprinkle flour onto a work surface. Put the dough on it.

5. Stretch the dough by pushing it away from you. Fold it in half and repeat. Continue doing this until it is smooth.

6. Sprinkle more flour onto the work surface. Cut the dough in half. Roll out one half until it is about ¼ inch thick.

7. Use a cutter to cut out lots of hearts. Then, lift the hearts onto the greased cookie sheets with a spatula.

8. Roll out the rest of the dough and cut out more hearts. Put them on the cookie sheets, then put the sheets in the oven.

9. Bake the cookies for 12-15 minutes. They will turn golden brown. Carefully lift the cookie sheets from the oven.

10. Leave the cookies on the sheets for about 5 minutes. Then, lift them onto a wire rack. Leave them to cool.

11. When the cookies are cold, draw lines across them with the icing. Cross some of the lines over each other.

12. Leave the icing to harden a little. Then, push in a silver cake-decorating ball where the lines of icing cross.

Christmas tree cupcakes

To make 15 cupcakes, you will need:
1 egg
1¼ cups self-rising flour
½ cup milk
⅓ cup margarine
1 teaspoon vanilla
2 teaspoons baking powder
⅔ cup sugar
baking cups
2 muffin pans
candy for decorating

For the butter icing:
⅔ cup butter, softened
2½ cups powdered sugar, sifted
1 teaspoon of vanilla or lemon juice

Preheat the oven to 375°F.

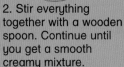

1. Break egg into a cup. Then, sift the flour into a bowl. Add the egg, margarine, milk, vanilla, baking powder and sugar.

2. Stir everything together with a wooden spoon. Continue until you get a smooth creamy mixture.

3. Put the baking cups in the muffin pans. Use a spoon to half-fill each baking cup with the cake mixture.

Stir it very quickly.

4. Bake the cakes for about 20 minutes and carefully take them out of the oven. Leave them on a rack to cool.

5. To make the icing, put the butter or margarine into a bowl and stir it with a fork. Continue until it is really creamy.

6. Add some of the powdered sugar to the butter and stir it in. Mix in the rest of the sugar, a little at a time.

7. Stir the lemon juice or the vanilla into the mixture. Try adding a little more if the icing is very thick.

Arrange the cupcakes into a tree shape, like this.

8. Spread some butter icing on the top of each cupcake. Use candy to make different patterns on each one.

Use a flaky chocolate bar as a tree trunk.

Wrapping ideas

Tissue twists

1. Cut a square of tissue paper or thin cellophane. Then, put five or six cookies in the middle of the square.

2. Gather up the edges of the square. Tie a piece of ribbon around the tissue or cellophane, above the gift.

3. Decorate the paper with small stickers. You could also try wrapping cookies with two colors of paper or cellophane.

Wrapping candy

Gift boxes filled with candy and cookies make great presents.

1. Cut a square of thin cellophane that is bigger than the candy, like this. Put the candy in the middle of the square.

Use a tiny piece of tape.

2. Wrap the candy in the cellophane and tape it. Tie pieces of ribbon around each end of the candy.

Gift boxes

Paint the inside of a gift box silver or gold. When the paint is dry, fill the box with lots of shredded tissue paper.

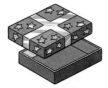

Lay a piece of ribbon across the lid and tape it inside. Lay another piece across it. Decorate the lid with stickers.

Cut a piece of tissue paper that is a little bigger than the box. Cut pieces in other colors. Line the box.

Find out how to make gift tags on page 64.

Tags and ribbons

A gift tag

1. Draw a holly leaf shape with a white wax crayon or white candle. Brush bright paint all over the cardboard.

2. Carefully cut around the shape. Write a message on the back. Tape the end of the tag to a present.

Ribbon curls

1. Cut a piece of ribbon 10in. long. Cut more pieces of ribbon the same length.

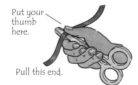

Put your thumb here.

Pull this end.

2. Hold a piece of ribbon between your thumb and the blade of some closed scissors. Pull it firmly.

3. The ribbon curls up. Curl the other pieces of ribbon. Tape them to the middle of a box.

DELICIOUS TREATS FOR EASTER

Chirpy chick cupcakes

To make 6-8 cupcakes, you will need:

    6 tablespoons self-rising flour
    1 medium egg
    ¼ cup sugar
    4 tablespoons margarine,
       softened
    paper baking cups
    a muffin tray
round candies and gumdrops
or other candy

For the lemon butter icing:
3 tablespoons butter, softened
⅔ cup powdered sugar, sifted
1 teaspoon lemon juice (from a bottle
   or squeezed from a lemon)
1 drop yellow food coloring

Preheat your oven to 375°F.

The cupcakes need to be stored in an airtight container and eaten within three days.

Decorate the chicks
with different-
colored candies.

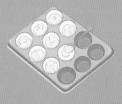

1. Pour flour through a sifter into a bowl. Break the egg into a cup, then add it to flour. Add sugar and margarine.

2. Beat the mixture firmly with a wooden spoon, until it is light and fluffy. Put 6-8 baking cups into pans in the muffin tray.

3. Using a teaspoon, half fill each baking cup with the mixture. Then, bake the cupcakes in the oven for 18-20 minutes.

Bake the cupcakes until they are golden brown.

4. Take the cupcakes out of the oven. After a few minutes, lift them out of the muffin tray and put them on a rack to cool.

5. For the icing, put the butter into a bowl. Beat it with a wooden spoon until it is creamy. Stir in half of the powdered sugar.

6. Add the lemon juice, yellow food coloring and the rest of the powdered sugar. Mix everything together well.

7. Using a blunt knife, cover the top of each cupcake with butter icing. Then, use a fork to make the icing look feathery.

8. Press two round candies onto each cake for the eyes. Cut triangles from gumdrops or other candy for the beaks.

9. Press two triangles into the icing on each cupcake, to make a beak. Make the pointed ends stick up a little.

Flower candy

To make about 40 flowers,
you will need:

2 cups powdered sugar

1 tablespoon lemon juice
(from a bottle or squeezed
from a lemon)

2 teaspoons egg white, from
dried or liquid egg white
(mix as directed on
container)

2-3 drops lemon extract

gumdrops or other small
candy

a small flower-shaped cutter

a cookie sheet

The flowers need to be stored
in an airtight container, on layers of
wax paper. Eat them within a week.

Use
non-stick
cooking spray,
if you prefer.

1. Put the cookie sheet
on a piece of wax paper.
Draw around the pan
and cut out the shape.
Put the shape in the pan.

2. Pour the powdered
sugar through a sifter
into a large bowl. Make
a hole in the middle of
the sugar with a spoon.

*If the mixture is a little
dry, add a drop of water.*

3. Mix lemon juice, egg
white and lemon extract
in a small bowl. Pour
into the hole in the sugar.
Stir with a blunt knife.

4. Stir everything until
the mixture starts to
make a ball. Squeeze it
between your fingers
until it is smooth.

5. Sprinkle powdered
sugar onto a clean work
surface and onto a
rolling pin, to keep the
mixture from sticking.

6. Roll out the mixture on the work surface until it is about ¼ inch thick. Then, use the cutter to cut out a flower shape.

7. Put a candy onto the middle of the flower, and press it down. Lift the flower onto the cookie sheet with a blunt knife.

Cut the shapes close together.

8. Cut out more flowers, and press candy on them. If a candy won't stick, dab water on the flower, then press it on.

9. Press the scraps into a ball, roll it out again and make more flowers. Leave on the cookie sheet for two hours, to harden.

Sticky Easter muffins

This recipe is based on cakes that are traditionally eaten in Greece at Easter.

To make 8-10 muffins, you will need:

½ cup soft light brown sugar
½ cup (1 stick) butter, softened
2 medium eggs
2 teaspoons baking powder
1 cup flour
½ teaspoon ground cinnamon
1⅓ cup (4oz.) finely-ground almonds*
4 tablespoons lemon juice (from a bottle or squeezed from a lemon)
muffin trays

For the orange and lemon syrup:
1 small orange
1 tablespoon lemon juice (from a bottle or squeezed from a lemon)
4 tablespoons corn syrup

Preheat your oven to 400°F.

You could serve the muffins with yogurt and fresh orange segments.

The muffins need to be stored in an airtight container and eaten within three days. Don't pour syrup over them more than two hours before serving.

Use non-stick cooking spray, if you prefer.

1. Brush some oil inside 8-10 of the muffin holes. Cut small circles of wax paper to put in the bottom of each.

2. Put the sugar and the butter into a large bowl. Beat them together until they are mixed well and look creamy.

* Don't give these to anyone who is allergic to nuts.

3. Break the eggs into a small bowl and beat them. Stir in the beaten eggs, a little at a time, to the creamy mixture.

4. Mix the baking powder, flour, cinnamon and almonds in a large bowl. Add them, and the lemon juice, to the mixture.

5. Mix everything well, then fill the holes in the tray 2/3 full with mixture. Bake the muffins in the oven for about 15 minutes.

The tray will still be hot.

6. Wearing oven mitts, carefully lift muffins out of the oven. After a minute or two, loosen their sides with a blunt knife.

7. Turn the muffins onto a large plate to cool. Then, carefully peel the wax paper circles off each one.

8. For the syrup, grate rind from about half of the orange on the fine holes on a grater. Put the rind into a small pan.

9. Cut the orange in half. Squeeze out the juice, using a lemon squeezer, and add 2 tablespoons of juice to the pan.

10. Add the lemon juice and corn syrup. Over a very low heat, gently warm the mixture, stirring it all the time.

11. When the mixture is runny, use a teaspoon to trickle it over the muffins. Let the mixture cool a little before serving.

Sunshine toast

You will need:

margarine
1 slice of bread
1 small or medium egg
a large cookie cutter
a cookie sheet

Preheat your oven to
400°F.

The toast needs to
be eaten as soon as
it's cooked.

1. Dip a paper towel into some margarine. Then, rub margarine all over the cookie sheet, to grease it.

2. Using a knife, spread margarine on one side of the slice of bread. Press the cutter into the middle of the bread.

3. Lift out the shape you have cut out. Put both pieces of bread onto the cookie sheet, with their margarine sides upward.

You can use any cutter that makes a hole that is big enough to put an egg in.

4. Break the egg onto a saucer. Carefully slide the egg into the hole in the bread. Put the cookie sheet in the oven.

5. Bake the bread and egg in the oven for seven minutes, or for a little longer if you don't like a runny egg yolk.

Use a spatula.

6. Wearing oven mitts, carefully lift the cookie sheet out of the oven. Then, lift the pieces of toast onto a plate.

73

Easter truffles

To make 12 truffles, you will need:

an 8oz. bar of white, milk or
  semi-sweet chocolate or
  1½ cups chocolate chips
4 tablespoons whipping cream
1 teaspoon vanilla
about 4 tablespoons sugar
  sprinkles
paper candy cups

🥄 The truffles need to be stored
in an airtight container in the
refrigerator. Eat them within five days.

1. Pour about 1 inch of
water into a pan. Heat
the pan until the water
bubbles, then remove
the pan from the heat.

Wear oven mitts.

2. Put the chocolate and
cream into a heatproof
bowl. Using oven mitts,
carefully put the bowl
into the pan.

3. Stir the chocolate and
cream with a wooden
spoon until the chocolate
has melted. Carefully lift
the bowl out of the water.

4. Leave the bowl to cool for 20 minutes, then stir in vanilla. Put the mixture in the refrigerator for 1½ hours, until it is very firm.

5. Put the sugar sprinkles onto a plate. Scoop up some chocolate mixture with a teaspoon and put it into the sugar sprinkles.

6. Using your fingers, roll the spoonful in the sprinkles to make a ball. When it is covered, put it in a candy cup.

7. Make more truffles. Put them onto a plate in the refrigerator for 30 minutes, until they are hard. Keep them in the refrigerator.

To make truffle eggs, squash the spoonful of mixture slightly when you roll it in the sugar sprinkles.

Marzipan animals and eggs

Chicks

To make 4 chicks, 3 rabbits and lots of eggs and carrots, you will need:

9oz. package of marzipan*
yellow and red food coloring
toothpicks

 The animals and eggs need to be stored in an airtight container and eaten within three weeks.

Wrap one half in plastic foodwrap.

1. Unwrap the marzipan and cut it in half. Put one half in a small bowl and add 12 drops of yellow food coloring.

2. Mix the coloring in with your fingers until the marzipan is completely yellow. Then, cut the piece of marzipan in half.

3. Put one half in a bowl and mix in a drop of red coloring. If the marzipan isn't bright orange, add another drop of red.

Keep this piece for the wings.

Press in two eyes with a toothpick.

4. Cut the yellow marzipan into five pieces. Make four of them into balls. Squeeze them at one end to make tear shapes.

5. Make eight small yellow wings and press two onto each body. Roll a beak from orange marzipan and press it on.

6. For the feet, make a tiny orange ball and flatten it. Cut the shape halfway across and open it out. Press a chick on top.

* Marzipan contains ground nuts, so don't give these to anyone who is allergic to nuts.

Rabbits

Use plastic foodwrap.

1. Unwrap the plain marzipan. Mix one drop of red coloring into it to make pink. Cut it in half and wrap one half.

2. Cut the unwrapped piece in half. With one half, make three balls, for the bodies. Then, cut the other piece in half.

3. From one half, roll three smaller balls, for the heads. Make six ears, three tails and three noses from the other half.

If the ears won't stick, dip the ends in water.

4. Pinch each ear to make a fold. Press ears, a head, nose and tail onto each body. Press in eyes with a toothpick.

Marbled eggs

1. Unwrap the second piece of pink marzipan. Add a drop of red coloring, and start to mix it in with your hands.

2. Stop mixing in the coloring when the marzipan looks marbled. Roll the marzipan into lots of little egg shapes.

Use orange marzipan to make carrots. Make marks on them with a blunt knife.

Press a rabbit's head on the front of its body, to make it look as if it is lying down.

Flowery cut-out cookies

To make about 10 cookies, you will need:

½ cup (1 stick) butter, softened
¼ cup granulated sugar
a small orange
1 medium egg
2 tablespoons finely-ground almonds*
1¾ cups all-purpose flour

1 tablespoon of cornmeal
8 tablespoons raspberry preserves
a 2 inch round cookie cutter
a small flower cookie cutter
2 greased cookie sheets

Preheat your oven to 350°F.

✿ The cookies need to be eaten on the day you make them.

* Don't give these cookies to anyone who is allergic to nuts.

1. Put the butter and sugar into a large bowl. Mix them together with a wooden spoon until the mixture looks creamy.

2. Grate the rind from the orange using the medium holes on a grater. Add the rind to the bowl and stir it in.

3. Break the egg into a cup and mix with a fork. Then, add a little of the egg to the creamy mixture and mix it in well.

4. Add some more egg to the bowl and mix it in. Continue until you have added all the egg, then add the ground almonds.

5. Put the flour and cornmeal into the bowl. Then, mix everything with your hands until you have made a dough.

6. Wrap the dough in plastic food wrap and put it in a refrigerator to chill for 30 minutes. While it is in there, turn on your oven.

7. Sprinkle flour onto a clean work surface. Then, use a rolling pin to roll out the dough until it is about ⅛ inch thick.

8. Using the round cutter, cut out lots of circles. Use the flower cutter to cut holes in the middle of half of the circles.

9. Squeeze the scraps into a ball. Then, roll out the ball and cut out more circles. Put all the circles on the cookie sheets.

The cookies turn golden brown.

10. Bake the cookies for 15 minutes. Leave on the cookie sheets for two minutes, then move onto a wire rack to cool.

11. Spread preserves on the whole cookies, as far as the edge. Then, place a flower cookie on each one and press it down gently.

Colored eggs

To make six colored eggs, you will need:

6 eggs, at room temperature
food coloring
wax crayons
tiny star-shaped stickers
rubber bands

The eggs need to be stored in a refrigerator and eaten within three days. They can be eaten with a fresh mixed salad or on their own.

Cooking the eggs

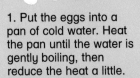

Use a slotted spoon.

1. Put the eggs into a pan of cold water. Heat the pan until the water is gently boiling, then reduce the heat a little.

2. Cook eggs for eight to nine minutes. Lift out one egg at a time. Cool them in a bowl of cold water for ten minutes.

Wax patterns

The wax resists the food coloring.

Leave the egg for about 10 minutes.

1. Using a wax crayon, draw patterns on a dry egg. Then, put 3-4 teaspoons of bright food coloring into a glass.

2. Half fill the glass with water, then put the egg into the glass. Using a spoon, turn the egg to color it all over.

3. When the egg is brightly colored, lift it out of the glass with a spoon. Put the egg on a paper towel to dry.

Stickers

Make sure the egg is dry.

1. Press tiny stickers onto an egg. Use shiny ones if you can, because they don't soak up so much food coloring.

2. Color the egg in a glass, as you did before. Then, lift the egg out with a spoon and put it on a paper towel to dry.

3. When the coloring is dry, peel off the stickers. You'll see the color of the eggshell where the stickers were.

These rabbits and chicks were painted straight onto the eggs with food coloring.

Stripes

1. Stretch a short, thick rubber band around a dry egg. Then, stretch one around the egg from the top to the bottom.

2. Add lots more rubber bands, then color the egg and let it dry. Then, remove the rubber bands to see stripes of eggshell.

Easter cake

You will need:

1²/₃ cups self-rising flour
1 teaspoon baking powder
4 medium eggs
1 cup and 2 tablespoons sugar
1 cup (2 sticks) margarine,
    softened
two round cake pans

For the butter icing:
2 cups powdered sugar
½ cup (1 stick) unsalted
    butter, softened
1 tablespoon milk
1 teaspoon vanilla

Preheat your oven to 350°F.

The cake needs to be stored in an airtight container in a cool place and eaten within three days.

To make the icing yellow, add a teaspoon of yellow food coloring at step 8.

Decorate the cake with flower candies (pages 68–69) and marzipan chicks (pages 76-77).

Use non-stick cooking spray, if you prefer.

1. Put the cake pans onto a piece of wax paper and draw around them. Cut out the circles, just inside the line.

2. Wipe the sides and bottoms of the pans with a little oil. Put the paper circles inside and wipe them with a little oil too.

3. Using a sifter, sift the flour and baking powder into a large bowl. Then, carefully break the eggs into a cup.

Be careful – the cakes will be hot.

4. Add the eggs, sugar and margarine to the bowl. Beat everything with a wooden spoon until they are mixed well.

5. Put half of the mixture into each pan. Smooth the tops with the back of a spoon. Then, bake the cakes for 25 minutes.

6. Press the cakes with a finger. If they are cooked, they will spring back. Let them cool a little, then put them on a wire rack.

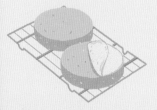

7. Peel the paper off the cakes and leave them to cool. When they are cold, sift the powdered sugar into a bowl.

8. Add the butter, milk and vanilla. Stir them together, then beat them until the mixture is fluffy. Put one cake on a plate.

9. Spread the cake with half of the icing. Then, put the other cake on top and spread it with the rest of the icing.

Chocolate nests

To make 10 nests, you will need:

an 8oz. milk chocolate bar or 1½ cups
    chocolate chips
¼ cup (½ stick) butter
2 tablespoons corn syrup
4 cups cornflakes
30 chocolate mini eggs or jellybeans
paper baking cups
muffin trays

The nests need to be stored in an
airtight container in the refrigerator.
Eat them within three days.

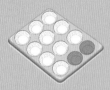

1. Put ten baking cups into pans in the muffin tray. Break the chocolate into squares and put them in a large pan.

The syrup slides off the hot spoon.

Try not to crush the flakes.

2. Add the butter to the pan. Dip a tablespoon in some hot water, then use the spoon to add the corn syrup.

3. Heat the pan gently, stirring the ingredients all the time, until the butter and chocolate have completely melted.

4. Turn off the heat, then add the cornflakes to the pan. Gently stir them into the chocolate, until they are coated all over.

Push the flakes up the sides.

5. Fill the baking cups with the mixture. Using the back of a teaspoon, make a hollow in the middle of each nest.

6. Arrange three mini eggs in each nest. Then, put the tray in the refrigerator and leave it for about an hour to set.

7. Take the nests out of the baking cups and put them on a plate. Keep them in the refrigerator until you want to eat them.

Easter fruit bread

To make a loaf with about 12 slices, you will need:

2 cups (8oz.) bread flour
½ teaspoon ground all-spice
½ teaspoon salt
2 tablespoons butter
1 tablespoon sugar
2 teaspoons rapid-rise yeast
1 medium egg and 5 tablespoons
  milk, beaten together
⅔ cup (4oz.) dried mixed fruit,
  chopped into bite-sized pieces
a little milk for brushing
an 8 x 5 x 3½ inch loaf pan

For the icing:
½ cup powdered sugar
1 tablespoon lemon juice
  (from a bottle or squeezed
  from a lemon)
¼ cup (1½oz.) chopped
  Maraschino cherries

Preheat your oven to 400°F.

Easter fruit bread needs to be stored in
an airtight container and eaten within three days.

Use non-stick
cooking spray, if
you prefer.

1. Put the pan onto wax
paper. Draw around it
and cut out the shape.
Grease the pan and put
the paper in the bottom.

2. Pour the flour, all-
spice and salt through
a sifter into a large bowl.
Cut the butter into cubes
and add it to the bowl.

3. Using your fingertips,
rub in the butter until
the mixture looks like
breadcrumbs. Stir in
the sugar and yeast.

If the mixture is too dry, add 1 tablespoon of milk.

Continue until the dough is smooth and springy.

4. Pour the egg mixture into the bowl. Then, stir everything with a wooden spoon until you make a stiff dough.

5. Sprinkle some onto a clean, dry work surface. Knead the dough by pushing it away from you with both hands.

6. Fold the dough in half and turn it around. Push it away again. Do this for five minutes, then put it into a greased bowl.

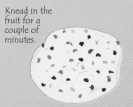

Knead in the fruit for a couple of minutes.

7. Cover the bowl with plastic foodwrap. Leave it in a warm place for an hour, until the dough has risen to twice its size.

8. Turn the dough out of the bowl and sprinkle the dried fruit over it. Knead the fruit into the dough until it is mixed in.

9. Put the dough in the pan and cover it with plastic foodwrap. Put it in a warm place for about 45 minutes to rise some more.

Remove the wax paper.

Use a teaspoon to drizzle the icing onto the loaf.

10. Turn on your oven. Brush the top of the dough with milk. Put the pan in the oven and bake bread for 30-35 minutes.

11. Push a skewer into the loaf. If it comes out clean, the loaf is cooked. Take the loaf out of the pan. Put it on a wire rack.

12. Sift powdered sugar into a bowl and mix in lemon juice. Drizzle the icing over the loaf, then scatter cherries on top.

Spiced Easter cookies

To make about 25 cookies, you will need:

1 medium egg
½ cup (1 stick) butter, softened
6 tablespoons sugar
1½ cups all-purpose flour
½ teaspoon cinnamon
½ teaspoon ginger
½ cup dried cranberries or raisins cut in half
5 teaspoons milk

about 2 tablespoons sugar
a 2½ inch fluted cookie cutter
two greased cookie sheets

Preheat your oven to 400°F.

The cookies need to be stored in an airtight container and eaten within five days.

1. Carefully break the egg on the edge of a small bowl, and pour it slowly onto a saucer. Then, put an egg cup over the yolk.

You will use the egg white later.

2. Hold the egg cup over the yolk and tip the saucer over the small bowl, so that the egg white dribbles into it.

Use a wooden spoon.

Find out how to make cellophane bags for your cookies on page 95.

3. Put the butter and sugar into a large bowl and beat until they are creamy. Then, add the egg yolk and beat it in.

4. Using a sifter, sift the flour, cinnamon and ginger into the bowl. Add the cranberries (or raisins) and the milk too.

5. Mix everything together with a spoon, then squeeze the mixture with your hands until you have made a dough.

6. Wrap the dough in plastic foodwrap. Put it in the refrigerator for 20 minutes. Sprinkle a clean work surface with flour.

Sprinkle flour on a rolling pin.

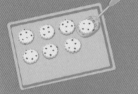

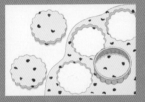

7. Turn on your oven. Then, put the dough onto the work surface. Roll the dough out until it is about ¼ inch thick.

8. Use the cutter to cut out lots of cookies. Then, carefully lift the cookies onto the cookie sheets, using a spatula.

9. Squeeze the scraps of dough together to make a ball. Roll the dough out as you did before and cut out more cookies.

Use a pastry brush.

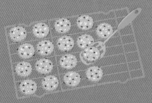

10. Using a fork, beat the egg white for a few seconds until it is frothy. Brush a little egg white on the top of each cookie.

11. Sprinkle a little sugar over each cookie. Bake them in the oven for 12-15 minutes. They will turn golden brown.

12. Leave the cookies on the cookie sheets for about five minutes. Then, lift them onto a wire rack and leave them to cool.

Easter daisy cookies

To make about 30 cookies, you will need:

¾ cup powdered sugar
10 tablespoons butter, softened
a lemon
2 cups all-purpose flour
writing icing or gel
gumdrops or other candies for decorating
a flower-shaped cookie cutter
two greased cookie sheets

Preheat your oven to 350°F.

The cookies need to be stored in an airtight
container and eaten within three days.

Use a
sifter.

1. Sift the powdered sugar
into a large bowl. Add the
butter and mix everything
together with a spoon until
the mixture is creamy.

2. Grate the rind from the
lemon using the medium
holes on a grater. Then,
add the rind to the bowl
and mix everything again.

Use a lemon
squeezer.

Sprinkle some
flour on a
rolling
pin too.

3. Cut the lemon in half
and squeeze the juice
from it. Then, stir a
tablespoon of lemon juice
into the creamy mixture.

4. Pour flour through a
sifter into the bowl. Mix
it in until you make a
smooth dough. Wrap the
dough in plastic foodwrap.

5. Put the dough in a
refrigerator for 30
minutes, to become firmer.
Sprinkle some flour onto
a clean work surface.

6. Turn on your oven. Roll out the dough until it is about ¼ inch thick. Cut out lots of flower shapes, using the cutter.

The number of biscuits you make will depend on the size of your cutter.

7. Put the flower shapes onto the greased sheets. Squeeze the scraps into a ball, then roll it out again and cut out more shapes.

The cookies should be lightly browned.

8. Bake the cookies for 15 minutes. Leave on the cookie sheets for two minutes, then put them on a wire rack to cool.

9. When the cookies are cool, decorate them with icing. Draw lines, swirls and dots. Press candy into the middle of the icing.

Cheesy chicks

To make about 15 chicks, you will need:
3oz. sharp cheddar cheese
1 cup all-purpose flour
¼ cup (½ stick) butter, refrigerated
the yolk from a medium egg
4 teaspoons cold water
a chick-shaped or other cookie
    cutter
two greased cookie sheets

Preheat your oven to 375°F.

The chicks need to be stored in
an airtight container and eaten
within four days.

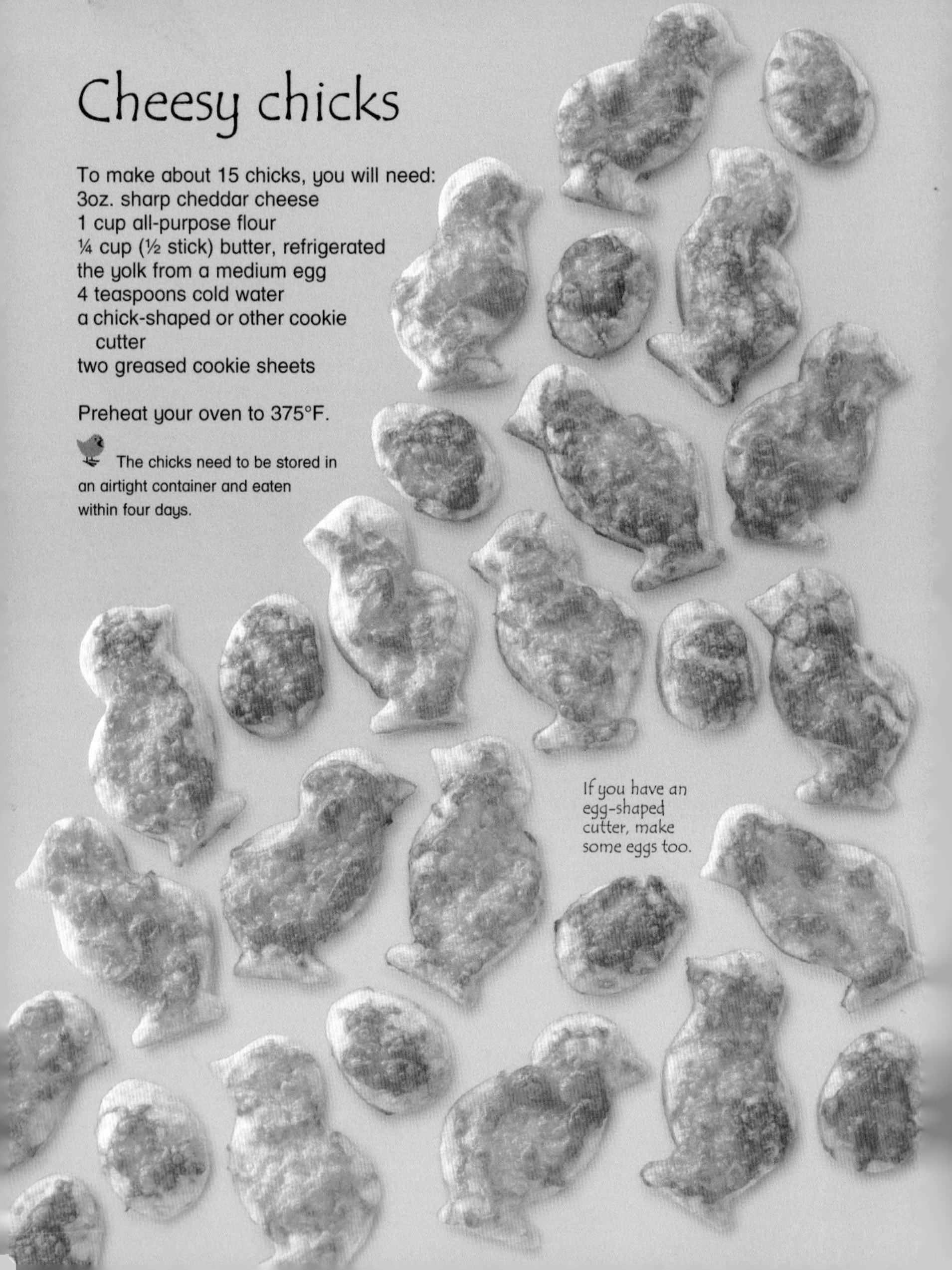

If you have an
egg-shaped
cutter, make
some eggs too.

Use the fine holes on a grater.

1. Grate the cheese. Pour flour through a sifter into a large bowl. Then, cut the butter into chunks and add it to the bowl.

2. Mix in the butter until it is coated in flour. Rub it with your fingers, until it looks like breadcrumbs. Add half of the cheese.

3. Mix the egg yolk and water in a small bowl. Put two teaspoonfuls in a cup, then pour the rest over the flour mixture.

4. Stir everything together, then squeeze the mixture until you make a smooth dough. Make it a slightly flattened round shape.

5. Wrap the dough in plastic foodwrap and put it in the refrigerator for 30 minutes. While it is in there, turn on your oven.

6. Sprinkle flour onto a clean work surface and a rolling pin. Then, roll out the dough until it is about ¼ inch thick.

Leave spaces between the shapes.

Use a spatula.

7. Use cutter to cut out chick shapes. Put them onto cookie sheets. Squeeze the scraps into a ball, then roll them out.

8. Cut out more shapes. Brush the tops of the shapes with the egg mixture, then sprinkle them with grated cheese.

9. Bake the chicks for 12 minutes. Leave them on the cookie sheets for five minutes, then put them on a wire rack to cool.

Gift-wrapping ideas

Bunny boxes

This side of the head needs to be on the fold.

1. Carefully cut the top off a tissue box and paint the box. Find a piece of thick paper the same color and fold it in half.

2. Draw half of a bunny's head, like this. Keeping the paper folded, cut out the shape. Open out the paper and flatten it.

3. Draw a face. Then, glue the head onto one end of the box. Glue a large cotton ball onto the opposite end, for a tail.

Pretty candy

1. Cut a square of thin cellophane that is bigger than the candy, like this. Then, put the candy in the middle of the square.

Pile candy or cookies into a bunny box as an Easter gift.

2. Wrap the cellophane around the candy and tape it. Tie a piece of ribbon around each end of the candy.

Candy bags

Leave long ends on the ribbon.

Put your thumb here.

Pull the end of the ribbon.

1. Cut a square of thin cellophane. Then, put several cookies or some candy in the middle of the square.

2. Gather up the edges of the square and tie a piece of ribbon around the cellophane, above the cookies.

3. To make the ribbon curl, hold it between your thumb and the blade of some closed scissors, and pull it firmly.

Add a paper handle to a box to make a basket.

Save food boxes and wrap ribbons around them.

Easter gift tags

1. Draw a rectangle on a piece of white cardboard with a wax crayon. Then, draw the body of a chick with a yellow crayon.

Draw an egg shape and fill it with lines and patterns.

2. Add a beak, a leg and an eye. Paint over the picture with runny paint. The crayon lines will show through the paint.

You can fill different areas with different colors of paint, like this flower.

3. When the paint is dry, cut around the rectangle, leaving a painted edge. Tape a piece of ribbon to the back of the tag.

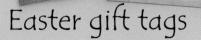

Managing designer: Mary Cartwright • Additional designs by Nicola Butler and Doriana Berkovic
With thanks to Katrina Fearn, Brian Voakes, Fiona Patchett and the Sales department at EDC • Photographic manipulation: Emma Julings
First published in 2004 by Usborne Publishing Ltd., Usborne House, 83-85 Saffron Hill, London, England. www.usborne.com